To Jess and Alice, for all the brilliance…
and the occasional tug of war! —*N.H.*

First published in the UK in 2017 by Frances Lincoln Children's Books,
an imprint of The Quarto Group,
The Old Brewery, 6 Blundell Street, London N7 9BH QuartoKnows.com
Visit our blogs at QuartoKids.com

Important: there are age restrictions for most blogging and social media sites and in many countries parental consent
is also required. Always ask permission from your parents. Website information is correct at time of going to press.
However, the publishers cannot accept liability for any information or links found on any Internet sites, including
third-party websites.

A catalogue record for this book is available from the British Library

ISBN 978-1-84780-850-9

Illustrated with lithography and watercolour
Designed by Andrew Watson and Karissa Santos
Edited by Katie Cotton and Jenny Broom

Printed in China
3 5 7 9 8 6 4 2

TUG
OF
WAR

Naomi Howarth

Frances Lincoln
Children's Books

One morning, while the sun was high in the sky over the banks of the great African river, Tortoise set off on a walk.

"It's so beautiful and sunny," he said to himself.
"I think it's the perfect day to make a new friend!"

The first animal Tortoise met was Elephant.

"Hello, Elephant!" he said. "Would you like to be my friend?"
"Be *your* friend?" bellowed Elephant. "No, thanks! I am the
biggest and best beast in this jungle, and you are nothing
more than a small, stupid old tortoise."

Tortoise walked away, feeling sad.

A little while later, Tortoise met Hippo.
"Hello, Hippo!" he said. "Would you like to be my friend?"

"Be *your* friend?" roared Hippo. "Are you joking? I am the toughest, most terrible thing in this jungle, and you are nothing more than a small, wrinkly old tortoise."

This made tortoise feel even worse.

Poor
Tortoise!

Now Bird couldn't help
poking her beak into
jungle business.
"What's wrong, Tortoise?"
she asked.

"No one wants to be my friend because
I'm small, wrinkly and stupid!" sniffed Tortoise.
"Nonsense!" squawked Bird. "Elephant and Hippo
might be big, but you are brainy. I bet you can think
of something to show them that being the
biggest doesn't make them the best."

So Tortoise thought…

and thought…

and thought…

until he came up with
the perfect plan.

"Oi, Elephant!" he said.
"If you think you're the best beast in the jungle, I dare you to hold on to this vine. We'll have a tug of war to prove it!"

"A tug of war with YOU?!" trumpeted Elephant.
"You must be as stupid as you are small."
But Elephant NEVER said no to a dare.

"Hey, Hippo!" Tortoise said.
"If you think you're the toughest thing in the jungle, take hold of this vine. We'll settle it with a tug of war!"

"A tug of war with YOU?!" hooted Hippo.
"You must be as silly as you are wrinkly."
But Hippo ALWAYS said yes to a fight.

Elephant took hold of
the vine and pulled on it
with all his might…

HEEEEeave

And Hippo yanked back as hard as he could…

"Heeeaaaave-hoooo, heeeaaaave-hoooo,

HE E E E E AVE

There was a creaking sound,
and then…

AP!

Elephant and Hippo fell flat on their bottoms!

How could they have been beaten by such a tiny
creature? They thundered off to find Tortoise.

But to their surprise, they bumped smack-bang into each other…

and in that moment they realised what Tortoise had done!

"TORTOISE!" they shouted.
"YOU TRICKED US!"
"You deserved it!" said Tortoise.
"Do you really think that just because you're bigger, you're better?"

Elephant and Hippo looked at each other, drenched
and dripping in sloppy, slimy mud.
"Elephant," said Hippo, "you look ridiculous."
"I doubt I look as silly as you!" said Elephant.

They turned to Tortoise…

… and burst out laughing!
"You might be small, but you're not stupid," trumpeted Elephant.
"And you might be wrinkly, but you are right," hooted Hippo.
"We have been the silly ones!"

"Tortoise," Elephant and Hippo said together, "would you like to be our friend?"

And from that day on, Tortoise, Elephant and Hippo *were* all friends, because they knew that no matter what their size, each of them had their own little bit of brilliance.